AF397233

Rasmus Selander

ME BOOK OF WRITTED THINKS

It's a Pine Duck

© Rasmus Selander 2017
Publisher: BoD – Books on Demand, Stockholm, Sweden
Printer: BoD – Books on Demand, Norderstedt, Germany
ISBN: 978-91-7569-698-0

Contents

Rasmus Selander is the author of this book.
Cover design, layout, drawings, photography (unless where noted) &
some title treatments by *Jacob Lindström*.
Some other title treatments by *Nemo Dahlén*.

This is the second edition of *Me Book of Writted Thinks*. This edition is longer than the first, but all of stories in the first edition are also in this one.

2017

An Happy Birthday

Harold

T'once t'was a fellow with name Harold whom when the fancy struck him would telegraph everybody he know and invite them to his tinny flat house for coffin and cake.

When the invitationed peedles came they each askingly told Harold: "Why oh why hath thou invitingly asked us to hither be gathered?" Harold then said he wasn't quaint sure but felt it an peasant gesture all the same. However soon he noticed that less and less pebbles were going to his department for coughing and jake. After a few tims of this no one at all came anymore, not one. T'is made Harold who was a norman happy lad into a compressed persian who no more liked to invite people so he never saw anyone, he just stayed at home and did not even change out of his pajamas.

On one day his tellingphone ringed. It were his uncle whom was calling. Calling to hear how Harold was as he had not ivittied anydobby for a time. And after hearing out his grandson, the uncle asked politely if Howard wouldn't like to come into his lard house for ccooffeess and cake. Harald said that he would. Upon standing at the door to his uncle's palace he knicked upon it and entréd. Inside then was every single person Harold had ever invented to his parties and as he stood on the mat. "Happy Birthday Harold!", they all shouted at him, and he was. Yes that day he truly was a Happy Birthday Harold and they all desided that every time it was his birthday they would do it again.

How nice!

Happy Birthday Harold!

• THE GREAT •

pirogue tail

In a town known to most as Christopherobbingham there long ago resided a merry band of businessmen. But these were no ordinary businessmen, indeed no mere grocers or merchant bankers, for their trade was in pirating. Which is to mean that they went out souling on the squimping seals to serge fer treachery and boots.

The name of their litre was Edward John Richard XII. It had been decided that he would be captain since he had not only the most buckles on his boots but also the farthest beard, what could wretch down to the floor. The other membranes of their crew were a man with a woody knee called rather fittingly Kevin. There was as well one younger bloke whose neame was Roger but he was always called Tom because of the state of his marriage.

Those three brothers-in-trade had during a long period of thyme made themselves known as the most fearsome, ferocious and most well-spoked pirates in the land and on the water. As mentioned they had been operating for some time so I shall render here their most adventorous adventure (so that you will feel like you're getting your money's worth).

"By the archbishop of Westhamshire would I like to go on one treasure hunt" said one day Tom to the crew.

"Good news then" said Captain Edward John Richard XII, "for I just traded my parry for this treshymap and it has a big cross on it and all!"

"That's no cross that there's an ekss." said Kevin who wasn't near-sighted.
And he was of coarse correct, and so they sat snail!

Their shimp was quite a bit bigger than most fishy boats but it was nonetheless a fishy boat (but with sales off course) and atop the mast was a flag with a skull and cross-bows painted on it so that everyone new they were pirates. They soldered on for many a days eating naught but seacucumber buttys and drinking only starboard wine. Ones day though they herd Tom shouty from atop him shrilly voice:

"LAND OH BOY AND ALICE WELLES!!"

For it was.

However when they had parked the boot they found not at all a big ekss like what had binned on the mop. Nor even a cross as Captain Edward John Richard XII had thought. Not knowing at all what to due they fastly found one of the only rehabitants and Captain Edward John Richard XII asked in his endowned pirating voice:

"Good day I am quite indeed very sorry to bother thou on a day like this particular one but you see wee three have a source of importation that upon your tinny inland shall lay an large ekks full of gold, silver, jooles and all sorts of valuable, comely things, won't you dear sir and or madame guide us to it for we see nowhere that might resemble such a space. We will be ever in your flavour if only you would be so kind as to lead us there."

The undressed man stood there gaping for a moment, rightly not knowing what to say. But after a whale he regained his speeching ability hand said.

"Eh, if you come 'ere looking for riches I'm afraid I cannot 'elp. Alls we've 'ere are these her pinapples 'n naut else."

The crew looked glummy at these worbs but then the person continued:

" 'Owever there to yer left's a great biggun island made all of treasures."

The Captain and his men turnt slowly but quickly in the way the woman said, and at ones their mouths went unclosed. The Captain tripped on his beard, Kevin's woody knee fell out and the state of Tom's marriage somehow worsened in disbelief. But then at that point when their wildest dreams came unfalse all in one go and they had a larger quantity of disposable income than they could indeed dispense with. An typhoid wind came and it made away with the merried men's fishy boat.

So then they were there thusly stranded on the sandy shore of an islington. But after a while they didn't really mind. For with their gold and jules they could have as many pinapples as they wanted. And who wouldn't want that? (They are an excellent source of vitamin C you know).

Sea end

CLAM GUTHRIE
AND THE
VILLAGE UPROAR

In a small seahorse village there was a fisherman idly fishing in his fishing ways. Most any time of the day he would be at his rod from husk til swan, except for mealtimes when he would walk up the dwindly path up to his cotty where he would eat together with his wife, who unfortunatley never left her spotty coroner of the kitschy.

One seeming norman day he went up for dinner and ate like he wood any other day but when he came back down the windy path and had walked out on the peir he found that his fishing stick had gone. However the man was not quick to anger so he spent the eve looking all about the pierre for his missing rod, but had not found it by the time his wife called out that supper was to be had. Slightly low in spirit he trundled up the path and sat down upon the table like always.

    - What's for eating luv?, he once asked her twice.
    - Stu, she said shortly and started eating.
    - You haven't noted my fishing rod anyplace for you see
    it went missing as we were having tea.
    - No, she said.

The day after the now non-fishing man went to the locale pleasemen to ask if the had sawn it or if they hadn't he would ask if them could not search for it. The pleesmen were helpful enough and said that they could at best put up notices on all the lamb posts in the village. *How nice*, thought the still non-fishing man.

A few days later however it turned out that the posters the

pleas had put up had greatly angled the towns postmen whose job it ordinarily was to tend to the posts. In outrage, every single one of the postmen had gathered outside the plishouse. The defective sargent was having abuse shouted at him by the Posty as the superintended of the posts liked to be called.

> - How would you like it if us postmen started going around helping people with their problems just because they say please! You wouldn't lick it one bit would you, so leave our posts alone! NYA! *(Or some such sneer similar to it)*

The Posty was so enraged with rage that he would not settle for an apology, he would only settle in court. So he called up his brother in-law who had a wig and a gravel and everything. It took many months to build a case, and they still didn't have anything to put in it so they took even more times. Finally on the 53rd of April the trial began. But it turned out so complex that the judge couldn't judge who was wright and whosn't. And some say that the trial is still going on to this day.

What about the fishy man whose pole was steeled? He never did find the culprit so it seems the pleasmen went through all that trouble for nothing. And the fishy man never fishied again.

Every story can't have a happy ending you know...

Delectable

Fedbows

Yes'um

Thank You

Indeed

Jeeves

Constabulary

There was a man whom was rather young for his age. He wasn't more than twenty though some said sixty-three nonetheless. He was not only incredolously ageless, as he was also very short and stocky. In fact he was so short and stocky that people laughed at him, not to his face of course (that's rude).

He had but one friend in this mortal realm where he had built a home, though he often complained about the view. This friend no one knew of so no one could really account for his existance. Moving on. His name was Milfred, he was a funny, dyspepsic, spastic, bespectacled old man who lived in a hat that our hero sometimes wore, though when he didn't he kept it on a shelf in his bedroom cupboard.

One day our hero conspired with Milfred about taking out his bottled-up anger on those who used to mock him, though he knew nothing about this fact, of course. They agreed that they would exact their revenge on the leader of this group (which happened to be a cult dedicated to a japanese artform known as hentai).

It was at the stroke of thirty-three minutes past four in the afternoon that their plot commenced. They snuck up to the caravan of the cult leader. (He was a redneck don't you know)... Anyways. They snuck up to his caravan really snookerly and knocked softly but softly on the door. He didn't answer so they decided to go in anyway. And they did.

As it turns out our hero was actually dreaming the entire time and was actually an norman peeple christened Dot, and she was always happy. That was because she was not real but instead just a thought in the deepesrt catacombs of the most secreted dugeon ever found on the thirteen C's of the made-up land of Nowhereinparticular. Which had been thought up by a middle-aged man named Dave.

NOT
a limerick

Trial and Errol were brothers
Though they did not resemble each other
For in moments of fear
You could easily hear
Errol the dim his screaming so grim
While Trial stood laughing beside him

It turned out that Trial but once in a while
Would play out a prank on his brother
Til one day so mad
Errol thought that he had
No choice but to murder the other

And so later I read
That old Trial was dead
Errol the younger
Had pushed him so hard
That the back of his head had exploded

And I didn't know
That to give rhyming a go
Would result in a verse
Which might make you worry
For concocting this folly
I truly am sorry

(I don't think I will rhyme again)

HELLO

Groobly Dershmant concludedly put down his morning paper with a sigh after realising that he in in no way whatever could decipher the small printed letters "Greb nud fernal trob" he said irritatingly to his wife, breathing loudly under his breath "Shre komt ure Grest" said she responively in an all- knowing fashion; for she had been there herself once

Groobly then without hesitation went into his study and slammed the door behind himself a few hours later he came out again looking alot happier than he had going in "Freb antralt veck!" he loudly excalimed and the dog started barking he then picked the paper back up and began to read it to his wife "ing rertur eftj" she said proudly and she meant it for Groobly had taught himself to read in only an afternoon isn't life wonderful children?

KEBIN
THE
SLUG

In a rather nice grassy sort of house lived a well-ordered family of slugs the youngest of which was Kebin. Kebin was not quite like the rest of his familing for he prefered the company of other animals to slugs, which was rather unusual and mead Kebin rather looked-down upon by his peers. (At least in this story.)

He had a group of friends existing of himself; Kebin the slug, a fox called Tim, a frog called Toad and a hedgehog called Cristopher. They were all close friends and used to hang out after school was over and they all got along really well.

However, one day Cristopher ate Kebin the slug along with his entire family of slugs. He claimed he did it by accident, having taken Kebin's invitation to come over for dinner a little too litreally. No one really blamed him though for it was only natural that he would have eaten them sooner or later what with Cristopher being a hedgehog and all.

Oh Well

TEETH

AT

MIDNIGHT

In the early owls of the morgan Pierce woke up to find his house besiged by an anvil deamon.

"What might your business be?" asked Peirce questioningly to the deamon. The deamon startled at boeing asked such a questionaire and so he spat (on the floor)

"By trade I'm the most well payed merchant banker in Blackpool you see" he said merchantly banking back and forth in the room.

"Well that's quite plain indeed" said Peirce quietly allowed.

"You're the only banking merchant in Blackpool, the man in the telly said so you know" said Perice not-knowingly.

He then went on to invite the most reputable banker in Blackpool to join him for his after supper morsel.

"So what brings you here" told Pierce the banker askingly.

"Oh you see I'm just trying to get a feel for this place" said the deamon bankingly, merchanting on a biscuit.

"How so?" asked Pierce in an asking manner.

"You see I have decided to start my own campaign to get into parliment and I am looking for voters, you see I don't have very many supporters yet but I really would like some."

"Sorry, I don't vote" said Peirce chokingly finnishing his teeth.

Unwilling & Unable

In the olden times there sat a man in a smoking room filled with peebles whom was all movie around in rythm to a tinny sort of nose emitting from a rotating, flat sphereoid. The man signed deeply, for he had a habitat of doing so. Then there came a woman nearby and started trying to pick him up but couldn't; due moistly to their distinct difference in body-size.

- Don't you wish to dance? she asked suggestingly the man.
- No I am afrail I was witheld the necessary information as to how one moves around in a coreografittied manner to musical accompaniment from the moment of my birth. Hovewer I am certainly certain there are plenty of other people currently in this establishment whom can do you the pleasure of sharing such an experience with you, but not I.

As the man looked around he laid notice to the fact that the woman who had appoached him was no longer there and must have been turned away at his exasperatingly long-winded and dull monophone dialogue. Satisfied with not having had to embarrass hisself attempting to pretend to seem to know how to dance he ordered another drink.

THE BIG YELLOW FOREARMED COCKNEY ARTHUR

A man called Arthur named Greg once woke up. He woke up and his big yellow forearms were all quite yellow indeed. (For he had three of each). He looked around himself and found that he had no idea where he was, because he had never been there before.

"Got meself in a right mess avn't I" he said aloud to no one. And no one heard. He got up from the place where he had been unawake and started to walk toward an opening through which sunlight was streaming into the rather cavelike thingy he was redcurrantly insinde.

"Now's about time for breakfast I'd think to miself" he said once he'd come outside; once again to no one. And no one heard. He looked at his watch, which he didn't have and noticed to his surprise that it was indeed ten minutes past whatever time it might be. For how was Arthur to know that it was really nighttime.

He had been walking for quite sometime now he thought; however that was not the case. He had actually only been walking for roughly four minutes. Suddenly he stopped. He had come to a small town that he thought he recognised, but he didn't really. In this town there was almost no one around, because no one lived there. No one except fot that one person whom no one liked, no one indeed.

At this point Arthur was badly flustered so he decided to follow his instincts which he kept in a small bottle neatly tucked in his left nostril because he thought that it was about the time he used them. And it was. They ended up leading him to one of the houses in which no one lived. He knocked five times upon the door, and no one answered so he went inside. When he had opened the door at once there appeared a rather small big cat. It told Arthur that he could not come inside becuase no one was there since no one lived in the house.

"Ey Kitteh I don't have the thyme nor do I have the rosemary for this so jus' go away ye" was his response to the cat's remark. For this really was the manner in which he spoke, that was why no one liked him very much. The cat however did not agree so he rolled over on his back, asleep. Quite. Arthur realised that he had walked into the kitchen, and he had. So he opened the refrigirator and started eating the food which no one liked, which was relish. Arthur loved relish, that was the reason why no one liked relish. And no one really did.

Once he had eaten all he could Arthur found himself getting rather tired of standing up and without a second thought he went into the bedroom to sit down on the bed. As he did so he fell asleep, right on top of the floor. Though the cat had said that no one lived in the house no one neither came nor left. Indeed no one ever found Arthur sleeping on top of the floor. Ever.

No one indeed.

RELISH

CRIMBLE CARROT

T'was around crimble time and everydobby slept
All the children merry with cheer listening with prickled ear
For old Santy and his rainy deer
Long about midnight they would come
And leave some presents for the ungrateful little brats
But old Nicholas he didn't mind
For he made his money on the side

So merry happy
Jolly Rudolph may it be a lesson
To everypimple young and olde
Appreciate all the pwesents that you get
Or you may one year wake to find
A stockinfull of Raindeer droppings

Merry happy crumble to all!

BILLY THE DOG

In a small Warwickshire village lived a dog.

Always he was happy though he did not have a home.

One day an man invitingly brought the dog into his house.

The dog then was even happier than before.

Or at least until there was a knock upon the door.

T'was the landlord come to say.

You may not keep an dog in here, never, not any day.

So let him go and don't you worry.

For by this time tomorrow I will have made sure.

That this dog will have been hit by a lorry.

This was not a very nice man.

BRIMBY GETS A JOB

It was a day like any other except for one small detail, it wasn't. Brimby had suddedly excited a building that housed *Pring & Fitzgerald Scholastic Agency* at witch he had been screamed for a job as a prep-school teacher somewhere in York. He thought it had gone no worse than most of his interviews (which usually didn't end with him getting the position). Brimby feeling high on spirits went about now looking for one place to have dinner, idly suckling down thick plumes of smote from the end of an littered cigarette (it was in the 50's you see and people didn't know any better). He stopped hestilly smelling a toothsome smell of chipshops and luckily walked right into one.

"Hello yes what do you want" said the man.

"Oh sorry but I'd like one lunch please"

The man smeared with indignation.

"I believe you mean one dinner"

At this Brimby started and blushed, begged the man's pardon and mubbered:

"Sorry yes one dinner please"

Brimby loved fishychips, they were his favourite actually. So he blisterfully enjoined every bit of it.

After having pained for his meal Brimby stopped off home where he lived alone. However when he came insinde he fount there was already somewon there.

"Hey there it is I Ronald Pyddlesnips!" announced the presence.

"Oh yes" said Brimby. "Sorry"

At that precise moment the phone started ringinginginging.
Ronald benign a gracious guess picked up the reciver and said;

"Yes hello it is I Ronald Pyddlesnips!"
Following this Minster Pyddlysnibs made from his mouthy grunty noses and put the talky bit of the phone back down.

"Brimby my dear fellow I have wonderous news for you, or my name isn't Rainald Eff Pydlesnups."

"Oh sorry, how nice." said Brimby.

It transpired that on the other side of the phone the talking man had been Mr. Fitzgerlad's secretery Ms. Palmywoodes to say that as Brimby had been the lone applicator for the post and the prebschoul peable were disperate Brimby had been heired.

Oh what an lucky time. Maybin we'll hear more of this another go.

Unsend

Mourning Retina

Randolph Greenflask the viscous vicar of Westminster begat whan (1) morgan by wokeing up. Slowly but slowly he made his way downstares into the kitchy where he brokefast at his own pace.

Laughter his meal he preceeded to finish off the rest of his daily route, finally staining in front of his mirror he squeezed his spotty face. After this ordeal he stubbled out to his car, and then he got inside of said car and went of to work. In a coal mine just outside of Wakefield, Yorkshire until his untimely death at the ripe old age of 58 and three quarters.

FIVE
SHILLINGS
A
MOMENT

One man a day found himself in the position that he was usually in, that is in a cardboard box outside a store selling all sorts of things really. The man had a name: Peter but everyone just called him Winston for short. Now the raisin for him spending his usual time inside a cardbroad box outside an all sorts sort of shop was, rather embellishingly because he lived there. But do not worry a bite for the box was a large box and even fitted inside it everything needed for him called Winston to do his business. His business being a accountant for a firm by name of H.N. Tellywink & Son's.

At any rate one dave he was enjoying his lunch-break coffy in his usual manner when a mann who knew Winston only by sight due to his beeing deaf in both ears came up to him and told Winstod in an asking sort of way:

 "I have it on goode austerity that you are an accountant, so I shall hire you to do a but of a counting for me, you see this here all shorts store is my propriety and I have yet to account for all of it."
Winston to this said with a mouthful of coffy:
 "I-I shall think about it, although I-I am pleasured by thyne offering I-I would say that you should in my stead go consider going to the accounter lacrosse the way as his fee is not what as large as my".

After sighing all of this Winston reached for a hankerchef, as he had in his expetidedness to answer a question asked of him that he hadn't rememberd to pidgeon his coffy and so it was now all over himself.

"Oh oh oh how incredulously wondering!" ejaculated the deaf all sorts fellow, lip reading. "I see now why you charge so much you see I had not ever accounted for that to be your andser; what may I ever pay you in?"

You see it was Winston's work as a accountmann to account for things his clienthell didn't.

"In money!" said Winston having a laugh.

finn

ADOLESCENT ANGST

(not mine though, luckily)

Mr. Mick Fitch, a young prodigy in the field of nothing in particular found himself on the bus into town. This was in no way peculiar or strange at all as he often did so. In front of him sat the infamous local reumatic and known spastic Mr. Trent, or as the youths knew him; Tremolous Trent the old loon.

Not being Caine or Able to stop himself Mick did as he always did and started tickling the old loon's few remaining whisps of hair, the loon thinking a fly was buzzing around him annoyingly brushed it away with his hand. Meanwhile Mick was laughing manically at the ridicule he caused the poor old fellow.

"That'll teach him for being sutch an owld loon" thought Mick. The bus then pulled up at the library where the young rascally rebel got of it and quietly laughed under his breath as he passed the stupid old man with his dum baldness and gross reumatism. It made Mick feel sick. Absolutely sick with disgust for the batty, strange old man. *Yuck!*

Gosh I am surprised he ever had any friends this Mick Fitch. It takes all sorts I suppose... Good Night.

Sad Jim

Once there was a man called Jim he was all sad like and was alone. He once put a wanted ad in the paper looking for a friend, it looked something like this:

6' tall, 35 lbs, dark-haired male looking for person of any gender to become friends with.
My interests include but does not exclude crying, self-pity, sobbing uncontrollably, being sad, sadness.
Favourite food: curry and chips.
Favourite colour: somewhere inbetween hot pink and magenta.
Call mc at 020-1210525136.

But Jim it seems was born to be alone.
Always Alown
Allways Aloan
Never

Thun Enk

morgan**comute**

It was quite a stormy day that I had the bittersweet mispleasure of for the first time meeting Mr. Richall Prompterdon. He was a man of stout heart and lager character than most. I had just boarded the train at Penningham for it was the one that went in the genral direction I wanted to go. Forward. Our exchange was absurd, almost comical and I have committed it to memory as follows.

"My dear sir, whatever do you think you're doing smoking in my compartment!? I have told the driver on more than none occasions to prohibit such erratic behaviour in my part of the train."
Baffled by such a piquant introductory expelling of syllables I replied as wittily as possible.
"My sincerest apologies my man but it is my view that one man's pleasure should not be hindered by another man's unconditional asthma."
The man I did not yet know as Mr. Prompterdon scoffed indignantly.
"How explicably thoughtless of you. Such an abnormally large head and nothing to show for it."
We continued to bicker and banter back and forth, exchanging pleasantries somwhere inbetween and before I knew it we pulled into Evertwumb station, which was as far as the train would take me.
"I shall expect your accompaniment again tomorrow!" Mr. Prompterdon said as I left the compartment.
And as I set foot on the platform it struck me that I'd forgot-

ten my umbrella that morning. Damn.

As it happened the following morning I had contracted a feverish cold due to my forgetfulness the day before, this occurance caused me to miss my intended train. I wondered then if maybe Mr. Prompterdon would somehow be in touch on account of me failing to rendevouz as we'd planned.

It greives me to say that he never was and that I never again got to have a second exchange with a man such as that. However it pleased me greatly to have met him and perhaps one day when I board a train I will bump into him again, or so I hope.

Signed dearly, *Sigurth Edwin Crinkly IV*

A Dead Inflated Follower of Fashionistas

Hello and be well-combed to this story I hope you will enjoy it as much as me had melting it. It stars Garfumbly Garfumbledon as Ravenous Rooney Longpipe.

It's the middle of an afternoon, though I am not sure which. Our hero is painstakingly staking pain as he attempts to dress himself for the great dinner party hosted by none other than the minister for dinner parties himself; Mr. Sir Mumblefred Mubbermurr. Dressing in the appropriate fashion of long socks and short trousers Rooney looks up into the strained mirror.

"Hm, yes I think that's done it." he says as he goes to the kitchen for a last cup of teeth before his great night indoors. He enters his fridge and then steps out of it somewhere completely different, handing the keys to a nearly valet waiting at him. "Very good Ser" he says.

Knicking knockingly upon the door he enters and finds himself on top of a big humble of pimples. "Ah!" says a voice behind him, Rooney looks up and and andsers "Oh Mr. Sir Mumblefeld Mubbermurr! I did not suspect to find your ear." "You found it!? It must slipped of my kneecap as I was making my way to the lavatory to read my papers. I've got four of them you know."

"My word your cauliflowers are really growing at a marvellous rate!" At this the minister takes of his porkchop hat adorned with cauliflowers and hands it to our hero.

"You can have them if you like, aubergines are the latest fad and a man has to keep things on top of himself."

At this our hero becomes rather shocked and stunned and wanders of somewhere else and enjoyed himself so much that he never left the party. Indeed some say he is still there, polka-dot suspenders and all. The End.

Pilchard Millagain

and the Matriculation Dinner

"Smett you Pilchard" said his mother allowed in an overtone to his father as Pilchard had ones agained knocked the jam jar to the floor. "Sorry mummy" he mubbered in his mubbering ways, at this his father grunted approvingly and said nothing more.

Then all of a suddy a knock could be heard at the front-door. Walking in without opening it came Jimmy Parsnips and what did he do? I'll tell you: "Good morning Mr. and Mrs. Millagain I just wanted te say that Pilchard should really be comming along as it's nearby time fer school and we'll be late otherwise."

"I suppose it's roundabout the time you left then Pilchard" said his father. "Okay then" said Pilchard boarding the train. He then went on to Eton and ate all he could have Eton.

Tre Bend

Hello, this is not the title of this story. Altough there are many strange and long titles in this wonderful book, this is just the designer of this book writing some stuff to fill out this page so it will not just be negative space. But do not worry my friend, the name of this story will be revealed in bold letters very soon. Live long and prosper. Now I shall let your eyes feast on the strange yet mesmerizing tale of **Lady Aberdeer's Rubber**

Edil an rather elderberry lady lived aloe but for her servants of whom there were plenty-three, in a large manor home in some "-shire" or another. The grounds were expansive and reached just about as far as you imagine with all sorts of flowers and paddocks and all the other things you associate with such a place.

As for Edil herself she was a once mary, thrice divorced ould leddy who now was rewired after a life of doing just what you imagine. She was waited upon instantly as she'd awake from her deep slumbers. She was of a rather frail disposition due much to her odd age; so much so that she had started to come apart at the seams. This little bother was upon each occurance remedied with paste, and smellotape for minor instants.

Edil's most favourite handler was stripy fellow with wery long wolly socks called quite splendidly Matthew. You see she was rather taken with Matthew, boeing particuarley enamoured with his wooddy socks. The ould ouman ould call espezally for the ladd in the mornings, for breakfast, dinner, and tea, and for moist other ocsillations really. And whenever he'd arride in all his wollyly socky spleendour she would coo and tisk and cajole in a lovvy sort of way which the man, Matthew plaid along with but really rather intestined.

Suddebly then arived one day a day upon which Matthew did indeed not show. No many how matter times Ebil would shoot and holly and when she ashed the other they all said in a sort of way "dnnu", shruggy ther shouldy and knot say anetheng else. Pour Edil never again set 'er dim eyes on the splendid Matthew with hiss long wolly socks.

35 years later it transpyred that Matthew had attempted rather successfully to run of with Edil's collective of home-hitted woodly socks. He would have most propaply gotten away with it if he hadn't confused to the crimcram in his bioautography.

Rather stupid really, just like you imagine.

THE
GOHST
WRITTY

Alone one evening in his flat sat a man at his desk which was covered by a jeep of crumply pisces of papyrus. The berson swore allowed and shook his head with annoyance. He got up and thought in presence tense that he could not in any way produce any descent work that knight. For you see this man was wan clever such for he was infamous for his writed storings. His moist popular wringing was those once what was scaring. He was blackcurrantly tying to witty a nother but thinking he couldn't. So he wet the bed.

Womever an unspecified number of hours later he awoke by the windy chill that swept into the room through the open windy. He gots up to un-open it when in comes in fast tense along with the breeze a translucent, shimmery sort of fellow who looks oddly white as a sheet, almost as if it was covered by one.

"I have come oh feeble humid to daunt you for I am a lost bowl who is forever left to not pass on to the next level."
"Oh how very interesting." said the man (let's just call him Everett W.A. Xyz Trousing) in an interested sort of way.
"I am very mildly interested as I am am author and write stories about just such creatures as you."
Everett carried on;
"Tell you what you write down your afterlife story and I will find a place for you in one of my cupboards were I can easily find a place for a lost bowl such as yourself. Do you agree?"

It did. And It sat at Everett's disk four owls, taunting him all the while (It was a host after all), until at first It said It was finnish. And so the man whom we call Everett picked It up and Carried It to the kitchen and opened the cupboard where he laid all his other bowls but just as he went to place It on a shelf he dropped it on the floor, completely by accident.

This as you might expect caused the lost bowl to shatter into many peaces, so many so that it would be very very difficult to mend. Even with industrial-stench adhesive. But Everett wasn't that displeased for he already had bowls to eat from and did not need another.

He later publicked the toast story and was poplar forever after.

Thi Ink

OH NO LOOK OUT!!!

A young lad called Ed usually went to school. Though he did not much like it there very much. This was mainely due to the fact that he was constantinpoley being burried by the other children on account of his not having any kneecaps. Ed didn't think it very faun at all having to explain to his mother Theresa why he returned home always with such filthy trousers but never had any friends. It got to the point where Ed finally decidered to never once return to school with all of its burying and none of its friendships.

So one early dave (the 4th of march to be precise) Ed tied some toasts, an jar of homemaid plum sauce and his portable gramophone in a hankychiff and slugged it onto the end of his granddad's walking stick, he then left the house. Leaving a reassuring knot to his pearants saying that he was only going to the chops. This was a cleaver excuse beacuse that normanly took Ed several hours as he'd no kneecaps.

He had gotten to the edge of the town, heading and footing toward the forest which was a nice forest; always sunny and smiling, unlike in books. He was whittling a tuna as he reached a small stream where he stopped to have a drink and a think. All of a suddy there jumped a nice old man out of a shrubbery and started splishing around in the stream. As this was indeed a nice man Ed wasn't scared two bits. Though he had gotten a freight when he first realised that the man was nude. Though as his grey shabby beard was plenty long enough to cover the most embarrasing parts of this story it didn't matter.

When the man noted Ed thinking on the brink of the forest stream he yelled out:

"But what might an eight year old boy be doing out here in no company but his own?"

Ed answered that it was none of the man's business, and that he was actually eight and seven months (he was very stingy around the topical of his age). The man however did not let up asking what Ed was doing by himself in the always sunny, smiling forest. Getting finally sick of the man's askings he said:

"I have decided to move away from here because I don't have a friend in school or out but it struck me that I have exhausted all of mine geographic knowledge and so I don't know where to travel from here."

"That can be easily melted" said the old man. "for I have a cottage nearby you see and in there is a map of the nearby areas."

Ed, delighted that the very nice man he had met wanted to help him on his journey gladly accepted and so they went up the opponent bank of the stream with the nice old man leading the way. As they kept walking Ed dicided to axe him how he had come upon a map as the man seemed rather to have no money thought Ed.

"Oh you see I was walking along in the sunny smiling forest when I came upon a man lying subconcious in the shruberry."

"Was he breathing?" asked Ed excitingly.

"No, no I am afraid he was quite dead." said then the moldy man and went on "You see someone had smashed his head in with a large, nearby stone."

The man shuddered as he uttered this horryfrying fact.

It transpired that the map had been in the dead man's hand and as the owld loon was a strong believer in recycling he had rather selflessly taken it. As the man's story wined to a malt they had reached his hut.

The inside of it turned out to be really pitch dark for there wasn't a window and the old man said he didn't believe in candles. He then started to dig around in the opening behind his bed, where it seemed like he kept what few objects he owned. Ed stood on tipped toes to try and see what he was doing when at last the odd fellow straightened up as much as his crooky back would allow. It was then that Ed noticed that the map clutched in the ould man's grasp was rather large, and roundish and it did seem really quite heavy to carry around.

Luckily Ed finally caught on and realised what the scrumpy old man was going to do so he bolted out of the hut as quickly as his kneecapless legs could move, screaming all the while. When he finally stooped the sun had changed it setting and Ed noticed that the naked old man was not longer after him. But then also that he was standing in a bussy town square. He had kept on running way past the forest and on through the next town which he had never visited before.

There was people pushing him around and walking in to him here. For they were adults so they only saw other grown-ups and not eight-year olds. Not knowing what to do Ed found himself drifting toward a side-street that had lots and lots of neon blinky lights and also many more adults. Some who were dressed rather funny. Really quite funny indeed for some of these people were almost as nude as the mossy old man Ed had met in the forest, but not quite.

These things all melded together led Ed to think that he had come to a circus, because he had herd on the radio that there were blinky neon lights and funny dressing people at circuses. Only; there did not seem to be any anymals at this molecular circus. Though just as he thought that very think there came from nowhere and everywhere a cacophony of noise consisting of loud sort of organic music and movements of massive foots.

And he saw suddenly coming toward him elephants in droves, but these were surely 100 times larger than any ones Ed had never seen. They were crushing the buildings as they went and leafing footstomps as big as creators in the cobbly street. One was just about to trample Ed, who had tried to run out of the way but could not move near quick enough since he had not kneecaps so he let out a horrible shrieky scream even worse than when he had run from the stoner.

Suddenley he woke up and looked around his apartment; it had all been a dream. A really livid dream... Scratching his stubby chin Alan looked into the camera and said:

"Fuckin hell mate."

MEET THE AUTHOR
RASMUS SELANDER

An unexpected interview via an online chat thingy

Hello Rasmus
Helo

What do you like?
hard questy

Name some people you look up to
J.R.R. Tolkien, Stephen Fry, Oscar Wilde, John Lennon,
Masatoshi Mashima, and many other

Who are you?
I am me

Which part of the human face do you like the most?
Depends on the face i think

*What time and place would you travel to if you had a
deleroan time machine?*
If I had unlimited fuel Stone Age probably but also
17th-Century Italy, 19th-Century London, 1920's-30's
Paris, 1950's New York or at least somewhere in the
USA, 1960's London and also Woodstock and probably Liddypool, 1980's Tokyo and probably some other
places too

If you were a superhero, what powers would you have?
I would want to have the ability of becoming fluent in any language of my choosing, not instantly though that wouldn't be very fun. Just quite quickly. That might be a boring answer though and not remarkable enough to be called a super power but it was the first thing that came to mind... If I had to choose something more traditional I would probably want to be able to control temperature

Your body temperature or external temperature?
Oh external

You've been given an elephant. You can't give it away or sell it. What would you do with the elephant? What would you name it?

I would feed it, take it out for walks, cherish, love and nurture it so that it becomes a respectable and kind elephant. But then I would realsie that no matter how much I care for it it would not have a very happy life living like that so if possible I would like to travel with it back to whiere it hails from and then see it safely released back into its natural habitat. The first name I thought of was Springy så I would probably call it that

(I apologise for any typos, I do not proof-read this)

I'm finding it rather difficult to put the answer to your next question into words but to try and not over-complicate things I would probably isolation. Because even though I tend to be sort of introverted however after an extended period of time in no company but my own I really want to see other people. Though as that answer will probably be to long and confusing maybe I should say that I fear death instead.

Why? And Thonk you. Is this for book propose?
It was fun.

Life is short. Stunt it!

Photo of R & J by Jonatan Eriksson

The team behind the book!
Jacob Lindström, Rasmus Selander (background)
& Nemo Dahlén (bottom right)

For more specific credits, see *Contents* page.

PIZZOAR

FSC
www.fsc.org
MIX
Papper från
ansvarsfulla källor
Paper from
responsible sources
FSC® C105338